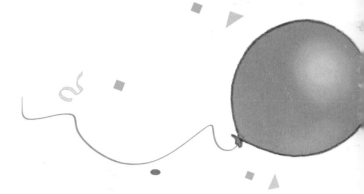

First published in 2015 by Hodder Children's Books

Text copyright © Mick Inkpen 2015
Illustrations copyright © Chloë Inkpen 2015

An imprint of Hachette Children's Group
Part of Hodder & Stoughton
Carmelite House
50 Victoria Embankment
London EC4Y 0DZ

A catalogue record of this book is available from the British Library.

ISBN 978 1 444 92456 5

Printed in China

MIX
Paper from
responsible sources
FSC® C104740

An Hachette UK Company
www.hachette.co.uk

I will love you anyway

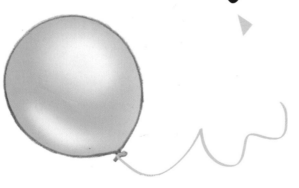

Mick & Chloë Inkpen

Hodder
Children's
Books

An imprint of Hachette Children's Books

I lick your face.
I bite your leg.
I nip your finger.
Paw your head.

I scratch the carpet,
Bash the chairs,
Dig the sofa,
Mess the stairs.

I steal your glove.
I steal your shoe.
I steal your socks.
They smell of you.

They tell me, 'Stop!'
They tell me, 'Quit!'
They tell me, 'Leave!'
They make me, 'Sit!'

I cannot sit.
I cannot stay.
I cannot fetch . . .

I chase a cat.
It climbs a tree.
I wag my tail . . .

. . . It chases me.

The days go by.
I run away.
(I ran away again today.)

I run away.
I run away.

I run away.
I run away.

They mend the fence.
It takes all day.
I find the gate.
I run away.

I **love** the park.
I find a poo.
I roll in it.
I look at you.
You tell me, 'Stop!'
You tell me, 'Stay!'
I run to you . . .

. . . you run away!

I chase the birds.

I chase a cow.

I DON'T CHASE CARS.

I know that now.

'He'll have to go,'
I hear them say.
'We cannot cop•
He cannot
'He canno
'H

tay.'

ven sit!' they say.

uns away!

We cannot cope!

He cannot stay!'

I wag my tail.
 (But I am bad.)
You smile at me.
 (But you are sad.)
And I am sad
 That you are sad.
You shake your head . . .

. . . and we are sad.

I run away.

The sky is black.

A drop of rain.

A thund

I run and

ercrack!

run and run and run and run and run and run and run and run . . .

. . . I don't come back.

I'm out
 all night.
I sit.
 I stay.

I wander . . .

 whimper . . .

wonder when . . .

 you'll come.

I don't
know where
I am.

Car! Car! Ca

Help! Help! Help!

Woof! Woof

Yelp! Yelp

Woof!

elp!

Squeals and howls!

And roars and growls!

And whines and wheels!

And what to do?

And then it stops . . .

. . . it's you!

You pick me up.
 You stroke my head.
You take me home . . .
 I share your bed.
I hear your voice
 Inside my head.
'Can I keep him?'

'Yes,' they said.

I dream of cars.
 I smell the rain.
I dream of cars
 Again.

If I could speak
What would I say?
That I will
Never run away?

There are **no** words
Inside my head.
I wag my tail
Instead.

I don't do 'Sit!'
I don't do 'Stay!'

But I will love
you anyway.

I don't do **words.**

They make **no** sense.

I jump for **joy...**

. . . and jump the fence.